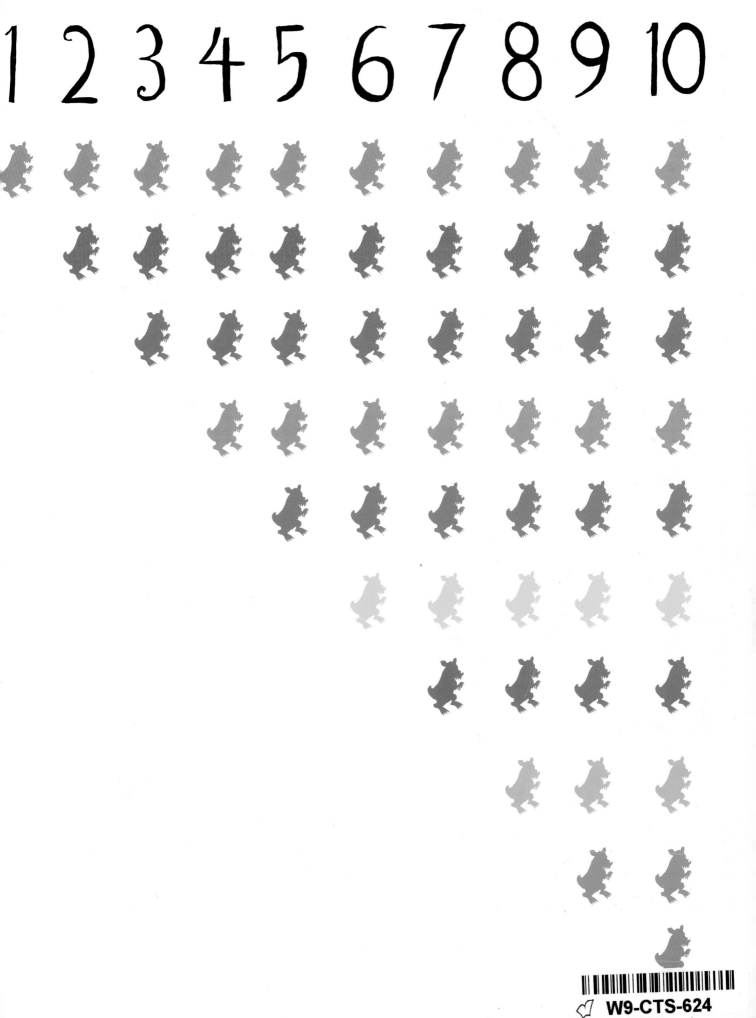

W9-CTS-624

Monster Hill

Monster
Team
TRYOUT
Today ↗

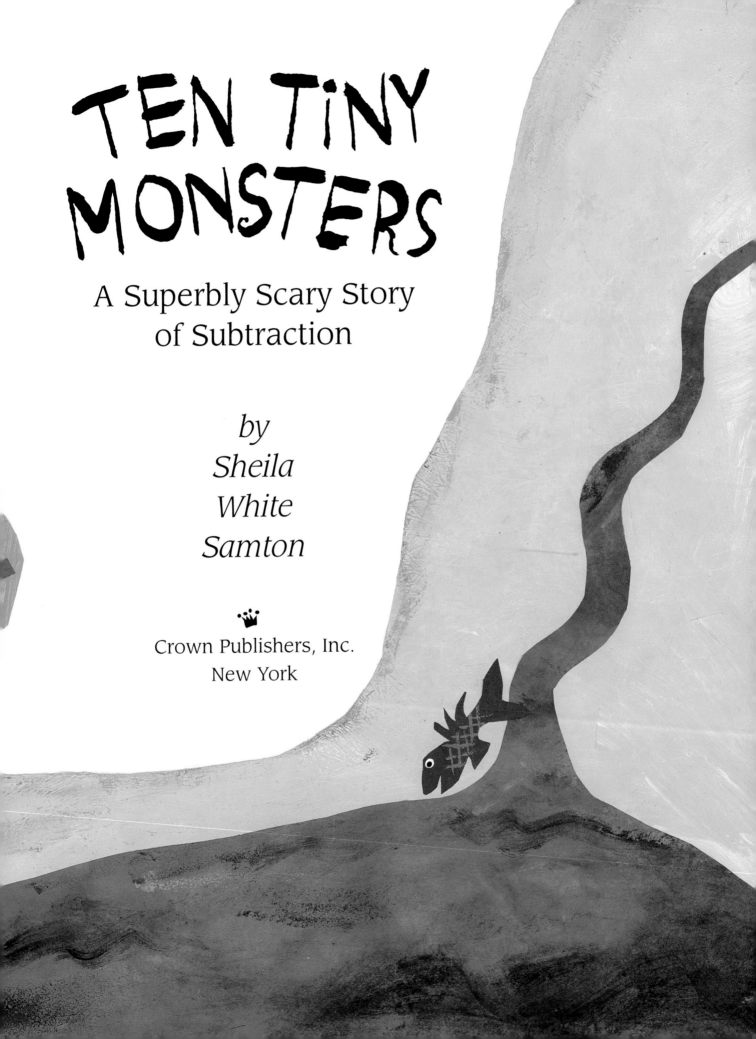

TEN TiNY MONSTERS

A Superbly Scary Story
of Subtraction

by
Sheila
White
Samton

Crown Publishers, Inc.
New York

For Cindy Horowitz, legendary monster-tamer

Copyright © 1997 by Sheila White Samton
All rights reserved. No part of this book may be reproduced or transmitted in any form or by any means, electronic or mechanical, including photocopying, recording, or by any information storage and retrieval system, without permission in writing from the publisher.

Published by Crown Publishers, Inc., a Random House company, 201 East 50th Street, New York, NY 10022
CROWN is a trademark of Crown Publishers, Inc.
http://www.randomhouse.com/

Library of Congress Cataloging-in-Publication Data

Samton, Sheila White. Ten tiny monsters / by Sheila White Samton
p.   cm. Summary: Ten tiny monsters try to make the Master Monster's team by finding something tinier than they are and making that animal scream with fright. [1. Monsters—Fiction. 2. Animals—Fiction. 3. Counting. 4. Stories in rhyme.] I. Title.
PZ8.3.S213Te 1997·
[E]—dc21   96-47355
ISBN 0-517-70941-4 (trade) 0-517-70942-2 (lib. bdg.)

Printed in Singapore 10 9 8 7 6 5 4 3 2 1

First Edition

Ten tiny monsters
stood in a line.

The Master Monster said:
"If you want to make my team,
Scare somebody. Make them scream!
Someone tinier than you,
Who will cry when you yell **BOO!**
If you can't, you'll take a spill
All the way down Monster Hill!"

Ten tiny monsters
Saw a puppy jumping.
BOO! yelled Monster Ten.
The pup jumped up—

SLOOP!

Monster Ten was bumped from the troop!

Nine tiny monsters
Saw a blackbird whirling.
BOO! yelled Monster Nine.
The blackbird swirled and twirled—

PLOP!

Monster Nine dropped off the mountaintop!

$9 - 1 = 8$

Eight tiny monsters
Saw a piglet wiggling.
BOO! yelled Monster Eight.
The piglet giggled—

Monster Eight received a push!

$$\begin{array}{r} 8 \\ -1 \\ \hline 7 \end{array}$$

Seven tiny monsters
Saw a kitten sitting.
BOO! yelled Monster Seven.
The kitten hissed—

SSSST!

Monster Seven was dismissed!

Six tiny monsters
Saw a squirrel scurrying.
BOO! yelled Monster Six.
The squirrel squawked—

TUT, TUT!

Monster Six didn't make the cut!

Five tiny monsters
Saw a chicken pecking.
BOO! yelled Monster Five.
The chicken tickled—

Monster Five went flying—one, two, three!

Four tiny monsters
Saw a worm squirming.
BOO! yelled Monster Four.
The worm wriggled—

YUCK!

Monster Four was out of luck!

Three tiny monsters
Saw a minnow swimming.
BOO! yelled Monster Three.
The minnow grinned—

SPLASH!

Monster Three left in a flash!

Two tiny monsters
Saw a bunny running.
BOO! yelled Monster Two.
The bunny thumped—

Monster Two had nothing more to say!

One tiny monster,
All alone,
Saw a butterfly fluttering by.
boo, whispered Monster One.
The butterfly winked an eye,
    Sighed a sigh,
    And fluttered on.

Ahhhh...

Tiny Monster One was gone!

The Master Monster swelled with pride,
And spread his scaly arms out wide.
"Every monster cub may dream,
But only *I* will make my team!"

"I'm the best! The one and only!"

"Still, it's getting kind of lonely . . ."